O9-BTN-560

Max Bonker
AND THE
HOWLING THIEVES

SOUTH
AMERICA

WRITTEN BY
SCOTT WEIDENSAUL & BRUCE VAN PATTER

ILLUSTRATED BY
BRUCE VAN PATTER

To Alison, who believed
(BVP)

For Connor
(SW)

Library of Congress Cataloging-in-Publication Data

Weidensaul, Scott.
    Max Bonker and the howling thieves / written by Scott Weidensaul & Bruce Van Patter ; illustrated by Bruce Van Patter.
        p.   cm.
    Summary: Max Bonker, adventure dog, sets out in his hot air balloon for the jungles of South America where he attempts to solve the mystery of the unhappy rain forest.
        ISBN 1-55591-244-3 (hc)
    [1. Dogs—Fiction. 2. Rain forest animals—Fiction. 3. Mystery and detective stories.] I. Van Patter, Bruce. II. Title.
    PZ7.W42573Max   1996
    [Fic]—dc20   95-54103
                                                            CIP
                                                            AC

Printed in Korea
0 9 8 7 6 5 4 3 2 1

Fulcrum Publishing
350 Indiana Street, Suite 350
Golden, Colorado 80401-5093
(800) 992-2908 • (303) 277-1623

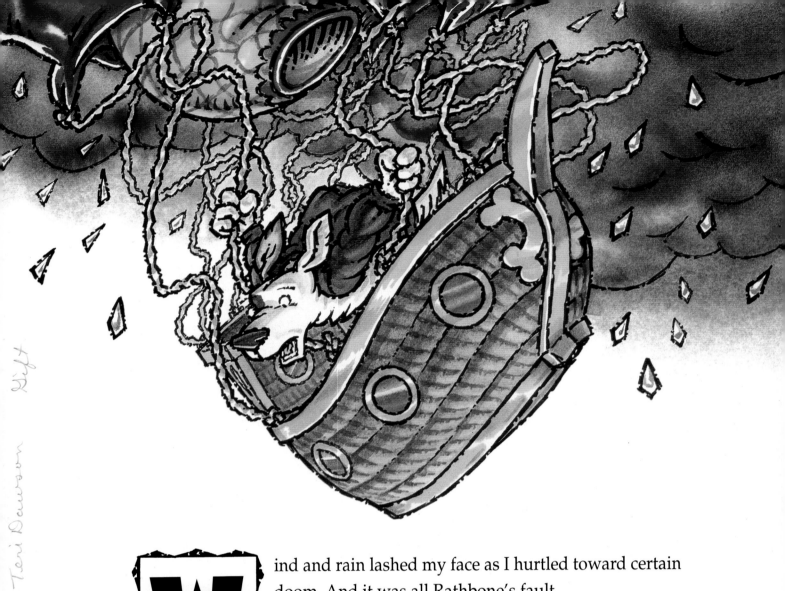

Wind and rain lashed my face as I hurtled toward certain doom. And it was all Rathbone's fault.

My name is Max Bonker, and I love a good adventure. So when I heard rumors that my old archenemy Rathbone was stirring up his evil brand of mischief deep in the jungles of South America, I set out at once in my hot air balloon, *The Golden Hound*, to stop him.

Far below me I could see the vast rain forest, with an enormous river running through it like a huge, brown snake—the Amazon, the mightiest river in the world. But as I came closer to the big island that was my destination, a vicious storm pursued me across the sky. When I started my descent in the roaring gale, a seam of my balloon split, and *The Golden Hound* went down like a rock.

The balloon crashed into giant trees, rolling me out into thin air. Only my keen reflexes saved me as I clung to a sturdy branch.

There was a rustle in the leaves, but I couldn't see anything—possibly because my eyes were squeezed shut.

"Lo-o-o-o-v-v-vely day, isn't it?"

I opened one eye a crack, peeking around. What looked like a clump of leaves slowly started to move, and I found myself face to face with the oddest animal I'd ever seen.

It was hanging upside down by its long arms, with fur almost as green as the leaves of the tree. Each of its feet had three long, curved claws.

"Why, you're a three-toed sloth!" I exclaimed.

"Of co-o-o-ourse." He looked at my feet. "But you're a strange sloth. A no-toe, perhaps?"

"Actually I'm Max Bonker, adventure dog, expert balloonist, and master detective, and I was wondering if you might tell me how to get down from here." He didn't seem to be paying attention. "Um, hello?"

"Beg your pardon," the sloth said, yawning. "Ju-u-u-u-u-st taking a little nap. I get so very sleepy. What did you say, cousin?"

This was starting to get annoying. "I'm not your cousin, and I asked you how to get down to the ground," I said.

"Down?" the sloth asked. "Why would you want to get do-o-o-own? No branches in the Lower World. No tasty leaves, either. All dark. Much nicer up here. But you've picked a ba-a-a-d time to visit, cousin. This is a very … unhappy … forest …" Drat it—he'd fallen asleep again.

I carefully untangled myself from the ropes, and despite my natural doggy dizziness from heights, I soon learned to move through the trees so gracefully that even the monkeys admired me. "Now," I said to myself, "it's time to see what kind of a place this is."

And what a place! As far as I could see, the tops of enormous trees stretched in every direction. Colorful parrots flew through the sky, and large butterflies drifted through the air. Even the branches of the trees were gardens, covered with a thousand different kinds of flowers and plants, buzzing with insects of every shape and color.

One bee zipped past, then zoomed back and hovered right in front of my nose to look at me. It was bright, shiny blue all over. I wondered if he might know anything about Rathbone's evil doings.

"Hello," I said. "I'm Max Bonker, adventure dog and master detective. Do you know if anything strange or unusual is happening on your island?"

"ZZZZZZounds! I sure do have a mystery," the bee said in a fast, squeaky voice. "My name is Bzz-z-z-z-tttt-zz-z-z-tt-zz, but you can call me Bzzztt for short. I'm an orchid bee, and we fly all over the forest canopy looking for a special kind of orchid that makes us smell good for the girl bees. One day I flew across the Great River just to see what it was like on the other side. When I came back today all the orchids were gone, and so were all my friends."

Being a fellow dog, Rathbone doesn't like heights any more than I do, so I couldn't see a connection between him and the missing bees. But a master detective never turns down a case, even when he's stuck on top of giant trees. "Tell me more," I said to my new friend.

"Follow me," Bzzztt said, leading me through the branches. "I know someone else with a mystery."

With a flash and a thump, a bird landed next to me, a bird with the biggest beak I'd ever seen. Bzzztt explained who I was, and she listened eagerly.

"Mr. Bonker, my name is Keeyos the Toucan. I eat lots of things—big crunchy bugs and little squishy bugs, wiggling lizards and slithering snakes. But mostly I eat fruit, which I pick with my magnificent beak. There's a kind of tree whose fruit I like best of all, but for some reason all the fruit has disappeared. It's a mystery!"

"How long ago did you notice that the fruit was missing?" I asked.

She thought for a moment. "Just this week. I flew to one of the trees to have breakfast, and there was no fresh fruit, just old, nasty rotten fruit. But I did meet someone else that day with a puzzle of his own. Follow me, and I'll take you to him."

We traveled for a long time through the treetops of the sprawling island. Sometimes I had to jump from one monstrous tree to the other. Even for an adventure dog, it was pretty scary—er, exciting.

We stopped in the fork of a great tree, where I found a tiny green frog with big, bulging eyes and sticky suckers on the ends of his toes.

"I'm Max Bonker. What's your name?"

The frog blew up his throat like a green balloon. Out came a trill so loud that it made my ears hurt. "Towering cumulus!" I yelped, covering them. "What kind of a name is that?"

"It's a frog name, of course. I have to be loud so my friends far across the forest canopy can hear me."

"Well, how about I just call you Emerald? I understand you have a mystery."

"I sure do," Emerald said. "I eat a certain kind of beetle, all shiny and black with little green squiggles. But lately I can't seem to find them, and I'm getting very hungry."

"Well," I said, "three mysteries is a lot to solve at once, even for an ace detective like me, but I'll try." So we set off through the treetops looking for clues, with Emerald riding on top of my head.

First, Keeyos took us to see one of the fruit trees. "This is strange," I said. "The tree has flowers, and it has old, rotten fruit, but no fresh fruit." Next, Bzzztt took us to where one of the missing orchids used to grow.

All over the branch, plants and flowers and moss grew, except for a hole where something had been ripped out. I studied it carefully. "Well," I said, "This gets more and more interesting all the—"

I was interrupted by a most peculiar sound. It started low, then grew to a great roar that echoed through the forest canopy, like a hundred lions growling at once.

"Violent vertical vortexes, what's that?" I barked, as the fur on the back of my neck stood on end. Emerald leaned over to my ear and said, "That's the troop of howler monkeys, Max. Stay out of their way."

The roar died away, and I sat down on the branch to think. The sloth was right—this was an unhappy forest. Orchids were missing, trees weren't producing fruit, and the little black beetles with green squiggles were gone.

I turned to my new friends. "Each of you knows a little bit about the mysteries, but there's a piece or two still missing. Who is the wisest animal in the forest?"

My friends suddenly grew very quiet. Keeyos looked over her shoulder, and Emerald cleared his throat a few times.

"Well," Bzzztt finally said, "you could ask, um … that is, maybe you could talk to …"

"Who?" I said, losing my patience.

"You could ask the Anaconda," Emerald said in scared whisper. "She's quiet as the mist, and she sees everything."

"You'll have to go down to the Lower World tonight," Bzzztt said, "to the banks of the river as the moon rises, and stamp your feet three times on the ground. Maybe Anaconda will come, maybe she won't."

"And maybe she'll talk to you, or maybe she'll eat you," Keeyos said. "Anaconda's *very* unpredictable."

I had to chuckle. "Come on, guys—you're not afraid of a silly little snake, are you?"

As it grew dark, I found a long vine and started shinnying down into the blackness of the forest far below. It seemed to take forever before my feet finally touched solid earth. It was so dark under the trees I couldn't see anything except the moonlight on the water just ahead.

There was a mist rising from the river, drifting through the trees like ghosts. But I steeled my nerves and stamped my foot hard. Then again. Then a third time, even harder.

Nothing happened.

"Humph!" I said, turning to go. "All the way down here for nothing! So much for the wise Anaconda. Just a lazy, fat, worthless … old … "

There was a slow, drippy noise behind me. I turned around reluctantly, and there I saw the biggest snake I'd ever dreamt of, rising from the water like the trunk of a towering tree. Water ran off the the scaly skin, making it shine in the moonlight, but Anaconda's eyes were shinier still.

I didn't make a peep. I just stood there like a statue.

Anaconda's tongue flicked out once, then twice. She lowered her head toward me, coming closer and closer. I wanted to run, but my feet wouldn't listen to me. Anaconda's huge head stopped just a few inches from my nose.

The great snake hissed a single word, like a jungle wind breathing in the trees. "Howlers," she said. Then she slid slowly back into the lake, and I didn't move until even the ripples were gone.

I climbed back up to the treetops, and the next morning I gathered my friends together and told them what I'd discovered. "I must learn more about the howler monkeys we heard yesterday," I explained. "Can you take me to meet them?"

Bzzztt shook his head. "The howler monkeys are a stuck-up bunch. They don't like anybody who's not another howler monkey."

"Then I'll have to go undercover," I said, "for I am also a master of disguise." So with some moss and vines and a gourd, I soon changed myself into a very realistic howler monkey, if I do say so myself.

I set off through the trees, following Keeyos, who flew ahead to find the monkey troop. The howlers were sitting around the branches, jabbering and scratching themselves and acting very important, but when they noticed me they all stopped and stared.

"Who are you?" the biggest of the howlers asked in a gruff voice. "I'm Cotomono, and I know every monkey on this island. I've never seen you before!"

"I'm Ma—I mean, I'm Marvin, and I'm from across the Great River," I said. "I've come to visit you, cousins."

It worked. The monkeys slapped my back and patted my head and poked my ribs—all of which just meant hello.

Cotomono grunted for everyone's attention. "It's time to get to work," he said, "and the Boss doesn't like to be kept waiting. Maybe our new cousin would like to join us." With that the monkeys headed out, swinging and jumping. I kept up as best I could. We traveled to a far corner of the island, and the howlers started searching carefully among the branches.

They were looking for orchids! One of the monkeys next to me found one with beautiful white flowers and gently lifted it up with the roots, hooting with excitement. As he did, little black beetles with green squiggles crawled out of the leaves. The monkey flicked them off with disgust.

Orchids? Beetles? Suddenly the pieces were falling into place, but now there was a bigger puzzle. Why were the monkeys collecting this one kind of orchid? I still had no evidence, but I did have a growing hunch that, somehow, Rathbone was at the bottom of this.

I had no time to ask. The howler troop was on the move again, heading for the opposite end of the island. Several of them cradled white orchids that they'd found. They swooped and leaped through the trees, coming down to a small thatched hut with a crudely built dock on the shore and a boat tied to it. I crawled down with them, trying to stay at the back of the group, out of sight.

A voice came from inside the hut. "So, my friends, what have you brought me today?" Hammering hailstones! It *was* my old nemesis Rathbone, that brilliant, evil dog. I'd battled his selfish schemes in the past, sometimes just escaping with my life. The monkeys were calling him Boss and showing him the orchids they'd collected. Rathbone examined each one closely. If it had even a bent leaf or a tiny brown spot, he tossed it aside. The perfect orchids he placed in big, special boxes divided into compartments—and almost all of them were full.

"Well done, my furry felons," Rathbone said. Then his voice dropped to a snarl. "But I'm unhappy you didn't bring me more."

Cotomono spoke up quickly. "We've been looking, Boss, but there aren't any of this kind left. How about some pretty purple orchids instead?"

"Fool!" Rathbone barked. "Knuckle-walking knucklehead! I told you before, the purple ones are common as dirt. These pure white ones grow only on this island, and my collection is incomplete without them."

Cotomono looked embarrassed. "Sorry, Boss, I forgot. Um … but could we get our pay for the ones we brought?"

Rathbone instantly became sweet and polite, the old faker. "Yes, of course," he said soothingly, handing out candy, which the monkeys gobbled greedily. The howler next to me sucked noisily on a piece. "This is good, cousin—even better than the fruit we used to snack on."

Fruit? Great gales! That reminded me of Keeyos's mystery. Suddenly I knew how everything fit together, so I crept off and rejoined my friends.

"It isn't three separate mysteries," I told them, "it's just one, and I've solved it. It all comes down to the orchids. The beetles that Emerald eats only live in those orchids—no orchids, no beetles. Bzzztt and his bee friends need the orchids to smell good for the girl bees, and when the orchids disappeared, the bees left the island."

"But why has the fruit I love so much vanished?" Keeyos asked.

"I think I know," Bzzztt said. "We orchid bees pollinate the flowers of the fruit trees, so when my friends left, there was no one to help the trees turn their flowers into fruit."

"That's exactly right," I said. "Without the orchids everything just fell apart."

"But what happened to the orchids?" Bzzztt asked.

"They are being taken by the howler monkeys, who are collecting them for an evil dog named Rathbone. And I think Rathbone is getting ready to leave, taking all the orchids with him," I said.

"This is awful!" Keeyos cried. "We have to get those flowers back somehow."

I nodded my head. "We'll need the monkeys' help to do it, and I think I know how to persuade them."

I went back to the howler monkeys, most of whom were sleeping. "Cousins," I said, "how about showing me this delicious fruit you've been telling me about? I'm getting hungry for something tasty." It took some coaxing, but finally Cotomono agreed and we trooped off to the nearest fruit tree.

Cotomono scratched his head. "I don't understand. At this time of year there's usually a lot of fruit on this tree."

I was about to explain it all when a horrible thing happened. I slipped on the branch and fell, barely catching myself before tumbling out of the tree. My disguise fell apart, and the monkeys howled in anger.

"Traitor!" Cotomono roared. "Trickster! You're no monkey. Get him, boys!"

I knew I was in terrible danger. Powerful hands grabbed me from all sides, preparing to throw me from the tree to a nasty death far below. "Wait!" I gasped, "you have to listen. It's about the fruit!"

The monkeys hesitated for a moment. "What about the fruit?" growled Cotomono. I quickly told them everything I'd learned—how the orchids they were collecting for Rathbone were important to the whole forest. "That's why there's no fruit," I said. "And when Rathbone—the Boss—leaves tomorrow, so does his candy. What will you do for food then? I need your help to stop him, and to get the orchids back."

"By my father's beard!" Cotomono bellowed. "He had us fooled—and *nobody* fools a howler. Of course we'll help you get those flowers back. And if we get our paws on Rathbone, he'll be sorry." So I sent a monkey to tell Bzzztt, Keeyos and Emerald to join us. Together, we came up with a plan.

Just at sunset, when the jungle sky was orange and noisy flocks of parrots were flying to their roosts, we crept back to Rathbone's camp. He was loading the boxes of orchids onto his boat, getting ready to leave in the morning. He opened the lid of the last box and gazed at the rows of perfect flowers.

"Lovely," he said to himself, "lovely and all mine. A new species, and I have every one. I believe I shall name it *Orchis rathbonis.*"

At that moment, Emerald's ear-splitting call rang through the forest. That was the signal! The howler monkeys roared loud enough to wake the dead, and Rathbone found himself caught in a shower of sticks, hard nuts and heavy gourds. Keeyos swooped in and out, bombing him with rotten fruit. Bzzztt zipped around his face like a blue whirlwind.

"Grab those boxes, you tail-draggers!" Cotomono yelled to the monkeys. They scrambled onto the boat and started hauling off the orchids.

Rathbone tried to make a break for it, but I cut him off before he could reach the jungle. "Bonker!" he said in amazement. "I should have smelled your handiwork, you meddlesome mutt!"

"Your plans are finished, Rathbone." I said sternly. "The orchids belong in the forest, not in your collection. Now you'll have to take your punishment."

But he just laughed.

"Catch me if you can, hound," he said, throwing dirt in my eyes as he jumped for the woods.

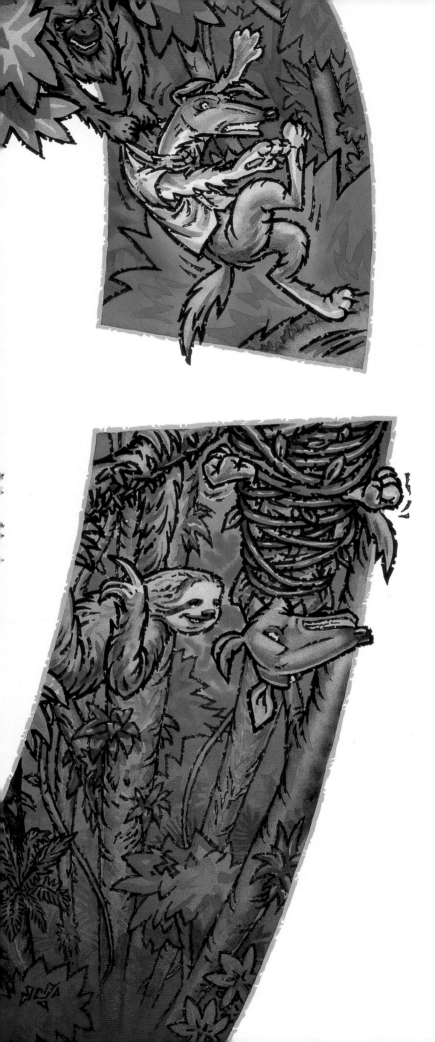

But before he could take two long steps, Cotomono's strong hands reached down from above and hauled him up by the scruff of the neck. "We've got plans for you, *Boss*," the howler said in an angry voice.

Hours later, as I worked my way back to the balloon, I came across Rathbone. The howlers had left him hanging like a ripe fruit, and I could see that the long drop to the ground terrified him. My old friend the sloth hung next to him, talking in an endless, sleepy voice.

"… and so-o-o-o I ate some leaves. Then on *Wednesday* I woke up and ate some mo-o-o-o-re leaves, and on Thursday I woke up and …"

"Get me down from here, Bonker," Rathbone hissed. "I've been listening to this mumbling idiot of a sloth for hours. You'll pay for this if it's the last thing I do."

"Not for a while, Rathbone," I told him. "You'll be hanging around here for quite some time, I think."

The next morning, beneath a brilliant blue sky dotted with butterflies, the howler monkeys were hard at work, this time carefully replanting the orchids on the branches. The smell of the flowers must have drifted far across the Great River, because soon Bzzztt's orchid bee friends arrived, filling the air with their buzzy laughter.

"It won't be long before everything's back to normal," I told my friends. "Soon there will be fruit for Keeyos and the howlers, and beetles on the orchids for Emerald. And Bzzztt, you and your friends smell terrific. The girl bees will be back, I'm sure."

Behind me, *The Golden Hound* was pulling against its ropes, newly repaired and ready to go. I jumped in the basket, waved to my friends and cut the ropes. Then I turned my nose into the wind, already sniffing for my next adventure.

ANIMALS YOU CAN FIND IN THIS BOOK

The **three-toed sloth** lives high in the treetops, hanging upside down and eating leaves. It moves so slowly that algae grows in its fur, making it green and camouflaging it from predators.

The **black-headed parrot** of the northern Amazon is often seen flying in small flocks making loud, screeching calls. Like many parrots, it feeds mostly on fruit.

There are hundreds of species of **treefrogs** in the rainforests of Central and South America. They are all excellent climbers, using the suction pads on their toes to keep them from falling.

The **emerald tree boa** hunts quietly through the jungle canopy for birds and small animals, which it squeezes to death before swallowing. It is not poisonous.

The **coati,** a relative of the raccoon, uses its long nose to sniff out food—fruit, insects, lizards and almost anything else it can find. It usually travels in troops, although males are solitary.

The **red howler monkey** makes one of the loudest sounds in the Amazon, a deep roar that can be heard for miles, usually at dawn. It feeds mostly on leaves and fruit, and lives in small family groups.

The many varieties of **passion vine butterflies** in the rainforest use their bright colors as a way of warning predators that they are poisonous to eat.

The **jaguar** is the most powerful cat in the Americas, measuring up to 8 feet long and weighing as much as 250 pounds. A silent hunter, its spotted coat makes it difficult to see in the forest.

The brightly colored **orchid bee** gets its name from the unique way it collects fragrances from orchids, storing them in special packets on its hind legs. The fragrance then attracts female bees for mating.

The **silky anteater** hunts for ants and termites at night and sleeps during the day curled up in leafy tangles. It uses its large, sharp front claws to tear open insect nests.

The **paradise tanager** is one of the most colorful birds in the Amazon rainforest. It searches through the trees for fruit and small insects, often poking beneath leaves and in cracks in the bark.

Able to use its long tail like a fifth hand, the **Brazilian porcupine** climbs easily through the canopy. Its quills are short but sharp enough to keep predators away. It cannot throw its quills.

The big beak of the **red-billed toucan** may look heavy and clumsy, but it is actually hollow and quite light. The toucan uses its long beak to pluck fruit from the tips of branches, out of the reach of other birds. The toucan also eats small animals.

The **scarlet macaw** is one of the largest parrots in the Amazon, almost 3 feet from its powerful, curved beak to the tip of its long tail. The macaw moves over huge areas looking for fruit and seeds.

With its long legs, arms and prehensile (grasping) tail, the **white-bellied spider monkey** can move quickly through the treetops. Spider monkeys travel in small groups high in the canopy, searching for fruit.

The **anaconda** is probably the largest snake in the world, sometimes exceeding 30 feet. It lives in and near the water, hunting for fish, river turtles, caimans (South American alligators) and other animals.